Visiting Elisheva

A story based on the Gospels of Matthew and Luke

AF235451

Stephanie Meier

2nd Edition November 2022

Cover Illustration by the author

This is the story of Mariam and Elisheva and their sons, Jeshua and Jochanan. I have related the story as it is told in the Bible (Matthew 1, 18ff and Luke 1), but I have also added fictional elements. I struggled a little with the description of the child being conceived through the Holy Spirit, and even toyed with the idea of making it a natural process. But in the end, I decided to keep to the miracle of the virgin birth, although this does not mean I fundamentally believe it to have been so. For me, it remains a possibility that the story is symbolic and may not have happened one to one as described. No matter how, it is still a good story — e se non è vero, è ben trovato!

Stephanie Meier, St. Gallen, 10th July 2018

© 2022 Stephanie Meier
Herstellung und Verlag: BoD – Books on
Demand, Norderstedt
ISBN: 9783756828142

Mariam strolled slowly along the narrow path in the early freshness of the Galilean morning. She was a strong young woman with lustrous brown hair and fire in her eye. At present, she felt able to cope with the changes occurring in her. However, she was aware that this positive feeling would not last. She had already experienced many mood swings in the last few days, her feelings changing like clouds moving across the sky.

She was grateful that Sarah and Shimon were setting the pace of their journey, leaving Mariam free to idle behind on the dusty path, and to ponder in her heart the astounding experiences of the past few days.

Was it only three days ago that she had felt such an indescribable ecstasy? In her own mind she called it the visit of the angel, to give the experience a name. She had been darning a gown and was about to put it aside when she suddenly stopped, both confused and excited. What was that sound? Where did it come from? It was like flapping wings or a rush of wind. She stood stock-still. Was she alone? Or was someone there with her?

A tingling sensation ran through her body from the soles of her feet through her spine to the top of her head. She began to tremble, unable to understand what was happening to her. Was she sick? The sound seemed to become dense, visible –

there, a face! An incredibly gentle, loving face appeared. Suddenly, she was no longer afraid, for she knew that whatever happened, the Lord God was with her. She felt the greatness of the Lord, within her and round about her. It was at the same time exciting and tender. Mariam was at peace and knew she was to carry a child.

But then, fear filled her heart since she was engaged to be married to Jossef. Their wedding was still some time away. What was she thinking of, to feel excited about becoming pregnant at such a time? Was she mad?

«Jeshua!» whispered a voice in her ear. She looked towards the gentle, loving face and was at peace again. Jeshua, why Jeshua? Yet there seemed to be no need for questions. She knew instinctively that the child Jeshua would be great, and important for the people of Israel and for the House of Jacob, to which her betrothed belonged. Mariam realised she was part of the great history of all being and knew that her holy child would be called the Son of God.

Her heart melted in love at the thought of the still unconceived child Jeshua, and a sensation of ecstasy threw her to the ground, hurling her darning work into a corner. Questions came again: How could that be? She had not slept with Jossef and did not intend to do so before the wedding. Yet she felt that conception would occur very soon.

Mariam realised she would never be able to understand with her mind, and she felt no need to do so. She was able to let go, allowing conception to take its course in its own way. Thinking of her child reminded her that her aunt, Elisheva, was also expecting a child. Elisheva's neighbours, Sarah und Shimon, had given them the news when they came visiting from Bethany. Elisheva was the younger sister of Mariam's mother, Hannah, and was known to be infertile. If God was able to plant a child in Elisheva's womb, He would also handle the conception of Mariam's child.

Mariam stretched herself out on the floor and gently stroked her stomach with one finger. What a thought — her child! She rose, put away the darning and stoked the fire to cook the evening meal, full of wonder at this new life soon to be growing inside her. Once she started going about her work, she noticed that the sounds of flapping wings and rushing wind had stopped. It was quiet once more, both in the room and within her.

2

When Hannah arrived home and began to help Mariam with the preparation of the lentil stew, she did not immediately notice that a huge change had occurred in her daughter. Mother and daughter looked at one another and smiled. A homely feeling of well-being spread through the small room. Not much was said that evening. It was as if Hannah knew that Mariam had something to digest.

Hannah recited the blessing, and they shared the meal in a peaceful silence. Afterwards, Hannah embraced her daughter who was looking beautiful, her face aglow. Mariam's great joy made her mother happy too.

Once darkness had fallen, the two women went to bed. But Mariam could not sleep. Lying on her back, staring into the darkness, she listened to Hannah's regular breathing.

All at once, the excitement returned. The darkness densified in places to form wings, hovering over Mariam. The sound of flapping wings and the rush of wind ushered in a similar ecstasy to that of the previous evening — ah, but now she felt no fear. Something great was happening to her. She had to place her hand over her mouth to stop herself from crying out! The feeling of ecstasy lasted for a long time, or was it only moments? Afterwards, Mariam could not tell.

Next morning, she felt nothing but shame. Who did she think she was? She was merely an ordinary woman. If she became pregnant now, a terrible taint would rest on her, and she would drag her family down with her.

When Mariam went out with a sullen face to fetch water from the pitcher in the yard, Hannah could no longer see any trace of her daughter's glowing happiness. Mariam was now fighting back tears — whatever would her betrothed say if she became pregnant?

Maybe it was all just imagination, maybe she would not become pregnant after all. But that now seemed even worse than the taint of being an unmarried mother, now that she knew about Jeshua and his great significance. Was she crazy? Was this all just a pipe dream?

Things continued in this vein for the next few days, until Mariam began to get on Hannah's nerves with her continual mood swings. When Sarah and Shimon came to take their leave before starting on their return journey to Bethany, Mariam suddenly had the idea of accompanying them and going to stay with her Aunt Elisheva for a while.

A mad idea, to leave so suddenly! There were preparations to be made, Mariam would require food for the journey, and her sleeping mat would need to be rolled and bound up. But once the idea had formed in her mind, Mariam could not be shifted from her decision. Hannah accepted the fact that she would be unable to dissuade her obstinate daughter from her plan. In the end, after the strain of the last few days and once everything was packed and ready for departure, they were both quite glad to part company.

3

«Come on, Mariam, you're such a snail!» shouted Mariam's travelling companion, Sarah, from the shelter of a group of trees where she was waiting with her husband Shimon.

«Yes, I'm coming!» answered Mariam, abruptly dragging herself back from her dreams into the present. She ran the hundred feet to Sarah and Shimon with long strides.

«Not so fast, Mariam, we've still got a long way to walk!» said Sarah. «You certainly never do things by halves, either you're a snail or a race-horse!» All three laughed, and Shimon leaned against their pack-donkey, Chital, who was waiting patiently next to him in the shadows, hanging her head in resignation. He smelt the sweetness of the figs she was carrying, merging with the warm, dry smell of the jute sack to a homely fragrance.

«Right, let's get on!» he decided, pulling Chital along by her halter, The little group moved slowly down the sloping path, stepping over scrub and causing loose stones to roll away under their feet with a hollow sound .

***

After a long march, they saw their day's destination, the small town of Nain, in the valley below, bathed in the golden rays of the evening sun.

«Made it!» said Shimon. «Now we just need to

find ourselves an inn for the night.» He stroked his wife's cheek lovingly. «You've coped well so far. I know you find the going hard, but we'll soon be home.»

Ahead they saw the town gates, tinted orange in the warm light. They found an inn, ate a simple meal, and Shimon and Sarah lay down to sleep. Mariam did not feel at all tired, however much her body told her she had walked far. Her mind kept dwelling on the events of the day, leaving her no peace. She leaned out of the window. Below her, two men had settled themselves on the ground of the courtyard with their musical instruments, one a simple violin with three strings and the other a drum. The small violin began a lamenting melody, the strains floating soulfully upwards. After a short pause, both instruments joined in a rhythmic quarter-tone melody, returning again and again to a pulsing refrain. Mariam was filled with rapture at the music. Her body swayed to and fro in time with the rhythm, as she raised her face to the crescent moon above.

The two musicians played for a long time. Mariam's eyes and body finally began to feel heavy. She lay down thankfully upon her pallet and was carried off by the wistful music into a deep sleep.

4

By midday the next day, they reached the main highway from the port of Caesarea Maritima to Skythopolis. Now they were no longer alone. Hordes of salesmen, caravans of camels, Roman legions, ox carts carrying whole families and countless nomadic shepherds were also travelling along the road. It was loud and dusty, making them feel uncomfortable. The highway was broad and well-maintained, but Mariam was jostled by a group of people talking excitedly, nearly pushing her into a roadside ditch. «Can't you be careful?» she shouted angrily, but the group were so loud and full of themselves that they were hardly even aware of Mariam's presence.

«Is everything alright?» asked Shimon.

«Yes, I'm alright, thank you, Shimon, but it's so annoying!» answered Mariam petulantly.

«Let's have a break,» suggested Sarah. «I've had enough too. We really need to rest.»

A nearby stream was almost dry and as there was no shade, they merely shared a brief, frugal meal and a sip of water from their water skins. No-one felt like a long rest with the noise and traffic. They had lost all sense of pleasure in the journey.

After the boring, grueling stretch on the highway, it was late afternoon when they finally saw the large town of Skythopolis in the distance. What a difference to the sleepy little town of Nain! As they reached the town gates, a large ox cart piled high with bales of linen was trundling out. They had to stand aside and wait, as the back wheel got stuck in a pothole just as it was passing the gate. The cart driver swore loudly, sprang down from the box and went to his oxen's heads. Together with several other bystanders, Shimon went behind the cart to give it a push. Finally it rolled on, and the cart driver climbed back up onto the box. Mariam und Sarah, who had been waiting in the shade of the town wall with Chital, joined Shimon and passed through the gates into the town.

They had to walk a long way from the gates to the centre of Skythopolis — the town seemed to be never-ending. They were tired and just wanted to find lodgings for the night, but the place was full of people and there was no room in the first few inns they tried, so they trudged on until they reached a tall house which was somewhat more expensive than Shimon would have liked. However, he realized his little group was sorely in need of refreshment and rest, so just this once he was prepared to pay more. The innkeeper explained where they could get a meal and where they could stable Chital.

After a delicious meal with sweet wine, all three sat in contented silence in the courtyard. Voices and laughter could be heard from the rooms of the house around them. The soft sounds lulled them, so that they had to force themselves to get to their feet in order not to fall asleep in the courtyard.

Mariam nearly fell over when she tried to pull Sarah up by her hand. The two women giggled like children until Shimon told them to be quiet. They were quiet until they reached the stairs to their rooms when the giggling started again. Shimon rolled his eyes in resignation. He would get no more sense out of them that evening!

5

Next morning, they crossed the river over a large bridge together with hordes of others who, like themselves, were on their way to Pella on the opposite bank of the Jordan. In the meantime, Mariam, Sarah and Shimon had accustomed themselves to the noise and the crowds on the highway.

Today's leg of the journey was fairly short. Mariam in particular was grateful for this, as she was feeling slightly sick. They found accommodation very early, and Mariam went straight to her room to rest. She slept almost immediately and for the first time, she dreamt that Jeshua was speaking to her, but upon waking she could not remember what he had said.

Sarah wakened Mariam for the evening meal, but she did not feel like eating. She would have preferred to continue dreaming of Jeshua. The excitement of the journey had almost made her forget the pregnancy, but now it became tangible once more. For the first time, it occurred to her that her sickness may mean the child was already in her womb and her body was dealing with the resulting changes. But it was too early yet to speak of it to Sarah. Her nausea could also be due to eating a heavy meal the previous evening.

However, next day as they wandered on along the left bank of the Jordan, Mariam suddenly vomited. She had not eaten much that morning. Sarah glanced at her with concern.

«Oh!» moaned Mariam as she cleansed her mouth. «Whatever's wrong with me? It must have been the heavy meal in Skythopolis».

«Well it obviously didn't suit you!» said Sarah. «I thought it was very tasty, and I have no symptoms myself, so it can't have been spoiled.»

Mariam dragged herself along. The day's journey felt like torture, although they were not walking through difficult terrain. Once they had crossed the boundary into Peraea and reached a group of trees, they stopped for a rest, and Shimon offered Mariam food and water.

Mariam drank greedily but did not want food. «Come on, Mariam, you've got to eat!» advised Shimon anxiously. «You'll see, it'll make you feel better. At least eat some bread, that's not heavy on the stomach.»

Mariam ate, and indeed she did feel better for it. She was able to walk all the way to the day's destination, a village on a hill, where they were staying with Shimon's brother. They were all grateful for the family atmosphere after the hustle and bustle of the big town, and Mariam felt happy again. She took part in the conversation, ate some of the simple, tasty lentil stew and stayed up longer than the previous night.

Next morning, they reached the River Jabbok,

where the patriarch Jacob had fought a battle with his God. Mariam was also secretly fighting a battle with her God, as the sickness had returned and she had to vomit again. She did not want the others to notice her sickness and break off the journey for her sake, so she attempted to put a brave face on it.

By now, she felt fairly sure the child was already in her womb, which was wonderful, but also frightening. How could she explain this to Sarah and Shimon, to whom she had become very close? She had no idea, so she tried to suppress the thought as best she could and to act as normally as possible.

The days of their journey as far as Livias were all much the same. Mariam sometimes felt like a sleepwalker, slightly remote from reality. Now and then, she lost control and became almost as cantankerous as she had been in Nazareth, after the visit of the angel. Sarah and Shimon stopped asking her what was wrong, as Mariam reacted more and more sharply to each question. But whenever Mariam lagged behind, supposedly unnoticed, in order to vomit, Sarah and Shimon looked at each other anxiously. Of course, Sarah had her suspicions, but she felt it was too early to express them as Mariam obviously did not wish to speak.

On the day they reached Livias, Mariam was feeling much better. Both she and her two fellow travellers breathed a sigh of relief. Maybe it had just been a slight stomach upset after all!

6

Two days later, an hour before sunset, they finally saw Sarah's home town on a distant hill behind an olive grove. Sarah sent up a high-pitched, quavering ululation which echoed across the hills. Mariam joined her in the jubilant cry, and all three walked the remaining mile of their journey at a brisk pace.

They reached the family's home in the dying light. Sarah's children were sitting outside in the warm evening air, rolling clay marbles down a self-built wooden slide. When their mother appeared out of the shade of the olive trees, marbles and slide flew in all directions, and they threw themselves into her arms.

«Hey, quieten down!» cried Shimon and smiled at his children, who smiled blithely back. «Have you been good while we were away?»

«Yes!» shouted both children at once. At that moment their old grandfather Jonah came out of the house and said: «They were little rascals, really kept me on my toes!» but his impish grin belied his words.

«That's not true, sabah[1], we were good.» Martha pouted and put her tiny hand in her grandfather's large one.

Martha was a proper little mother; although

---

[1] Hebrew for grandad

she was only five years old she liked to take care of the housework and to boss her little brother Elazar around. Jonah's task of looking after the children and the house during Sarah's and Shimon's travels over the last five weeks had not been so strenuous.

As the sun became a fireball on the horizon, Sarah remembered her responsibility as Mariam's hostess. «Here's Hannah's daughter, Mariam, come to visit us! This is my father-in-law Jonah, and our two children Martha and Elazar.» Everyone turned to look at Mariam, who stepped into the midst of the friendly family and greeted each one with a glowing smile.

«Right, let's go into the house!» said Shimon. «Children, you can bring Chital to her stable. And don't forget to rub her down and give her a bucket of water, for she's worked very hard!» Shimon removed the sacks of almonds and dried figs from her back and stored them in an outhouse, then everyone went into the living room, while the children toddled off happily and noisily towards the stable, leading Chital by her leather halter.

They were welcomed by the homely smell of the oil lamps Sarah had lit. The family sat together with Mariam on a circle of cushions on the floor. They exchanged news, and Sarah and Shimon told Jonah all about the journey to and from Nazareth.

After a while, Sarah got up to do some housework. «Will you be going to Elisheva tomorrow already, Mariam?» she asked

«I'd certainly like to let her know I'm here. But may I come back and spend another three nights with you? Elisheva's not prepared for my visit. The day after tomorrow is Schabbat and she'll need time to get everything ready. Of course I'll help her with all I can. But I feel it'll be easier for her if I can spend three more nights with you.»

«You're absolutely right. That's an excellent idea, and of course you're very welcome to stay with us as long as you like. On the contrary, I believe I'll miss you very much!» The two women embraced. They had become close on the journey, and Sarah brushed away a tear.

Mariam tenderley touched her cheek. «I'll miss you too, Sarah! Thanks for everything.»

Mariam also felt tears pricking her eyes. She went into her bedroom and sobbed violently. All the emotions of the past week suddenly broke their bounds and could no longer be suppressed. She was looking forward so much to seeing Elisheva, as she would finally be able to tell her all that had happened. Sarah was kind. Mariam was fond of her, but she was not family and Mariam could not expect her to understand the situation she was in. It then occurred to her that she could not expect her family to understand it either. However, she sensed that with Elisheva, everything was going to be different.

7

Mariam cried herself to sleep and slept long and deeply. Sarah looked in on her early, but Mariam was sleeping so peacefully that she did not wake her. After saying morning prayer together, Mariam only ate a light breakfast. She was far too excited to eat properly and sat pensively at the table, looking serious.

Finally she got up, taking the sack of dates she had brought from Nazareth as a present for Elisheva and her husband Zecharijas, took her leave of Sarah and made her way to Elisheva's house nearby.

She felt nervous as she knocked on the door. Elisheva opened it and stood there looking very surprised, her hands pressed into her back to support her growing belly.

«Elisheva!» exclaimed Mariam, «God has blessed you!»

Elisheva looked down at her belly, and a dignified smile lit her face, for her child had moved so distinctly in her womb that even Mariam had seen it!

«Mariam, my dear niece!» exclaimed Elisheva and took Mariam in her arms. «Come in! What a surprise!»

Elisheva held Mariam's arm and looked at her in amazement. «Mariam, how you've changed. I see you've also been blessed by God, and the child growing inside you is still more blessed!»

Mariam's eyes grew round with surprise. She sat down suddenly. «You can see that, Elisheva?»

«God must have told me,» answered Elisheva, who was even more surprised by her own words than Mariam. But Mariam's reply confirmed that she was right. «Why am I so favoured, that the mother of my Lord has come to me?» she continued, and marvelled again at her own words. «You saw that my child moved when you greeted me. He felt it too — your child will be great, he will be the Lord of us all!»

Mariam heard the soft beating of wings and the rush of wind as Elisheva spoke. Her heart seemed to overflow. She stood up as emotion took hold of her, and began to recite words from the Scriptures, from the first book of Samuel, from the Psalms, from Isaiah and from other books proclaiming God's promise for Israel — her child was now a part of that promise.

Beginning softly, she recited ever more strongly:

«My soul glorifies the Lord
and my spirit rejoices in God my Saviour,
for he has been mindful of the humble state of his servant.
From now on all generations will call me blessed,
for the Mighty One has done great things for me — holy is his name.
His mercy extends to those who fear him, from

generation to generation.

He has performed mighty deeds with his arm;
He has scattered those who are proud in their
inmost thoughts.

He has brought down rulers from their thrones
but has lifted up the humble.

He has filled the hungry with good things but
has sent the rich away empty.

He has helped his servant Israel, remembering
to be merciful to Abraham and his descendants
forever, just as he promised our ancestors.[2]»

Elisheva stood beside her the whole time, watching her with wonder and awe. She could sense that both of their children were to be a part of God's promise, and would be counted with the greatest in the history of Israel. As Mariam's voice faded on the last note of the song, the beating of wings and the rush of wind faded with it. The two women looked each other in the eye. What was happening to them both was clearly a miracle, and there was no more need for words, only silent acceptance.

They heard steps at the door as Zecharijas entered. Elisheva exclaimed: «Zecharijas, just look who's come to visit us — my niece Mariam from Nazareth!»

Zecharijas looked at Mariam and gave a slight bow, but he said nothing. Elisheva explained: «Since

---

[2] Luke 1, 46-55

I became pregnant, Zecharijas has lost his voice completely.»

Mariam regarded Zecharijas with concern, but Elisheva passed him a wax tablet and a stylus, and he wrote: «Welcome, Mariam! Have you come here to help Elisheva?»

Mariam smiled. «That's exactly what I'll be doing in the next few weeks, yes! And if it's alright with you, I'd like to stay here. But only in three days' time. Until then I'll be staying with your neighbours, Sarah and Shimon, with whom I travelled from Nazareth. Elisheva, I'll gladly help you with everything I can!»

«Of course you must stay with us!» Elisheva was thrilled. She would have preferred not to let Mariam return to her neighbours. However, once they had done all the preparations for the Sabbath and Mariam had returned to Shimon and Sarah, Elisheva already felt quite tired and was glad of some peace and quiet in which to assimilate all that had happened.

8

After the Sabbath, Elisheva was unable to sleep from excitement, and the still of the night gave her the opportunity to think things through. She was convinced of the divine nature of the child in Mariam's womb, but how had it come to pass? Her own child was also a divine gift and destined for greatness, yet she knew that the gift had been bestowed through natural conception by her husband Zecharijas. With Mariam it was quite a different matter. She was a young, single woman engaged to be married to Jossef, but she should not yet have had intercourse with him.

The consequences for Mariam's life were predictable and could not be good. At present, she was safe with Elisheva, but as soon as she returned home, her problems would only just begin. Elisheva sensed that Mariam had not yet spoken to anyone about her pregnancy.

Thus it was that next morning, Elisheva opened the door to Mariam's knock with a frown. She led her to the table and gave her a beaker of water to drink.

«I really am pleased to see you, Mariam. But I must ask you — was the child conceived by Jossef?»

Mariam sensed with misgiving how often she would be asked this question. At present, although it was a formidable prospect, she did not yet feel fear, as it was all too distant and unreal.

«No,» she replied, «the child's not Jossef's.»

Elisheva's eyes opened wide. «Whose is it then?» she asked, aghast.

«Elisheva, I have not slept with a man.»

«How can that happen, then?»

«Do you believe in miracles? This is a miracle.»

«Yes, of course. My pregnancy is a miracle, I'm really too old, but ….» Elisheva left the sentence unfinished, confused and perplexed. This was too high for her!

The women sat still for a few moments in pondering silence .

«When I realised I was going to conceive a child,» continued Elisheva, «there was a curious atmosphere, and I heard a soft sound, like beating wings and a rush of wind in the chamber, although there's no window to let in air.»

«That's exactly the same as it was for me!» interrupted Mariam. «Beating wings and the rush of wind, that's exactly how it sounded. And yesterday evening as I came to you, I heard it again.»

«Yes, so did I. That's significant. It's a sign that it comes from God. Yesterday evening, it seemed to me that our two children were able to communicate with each other through the walls of our bellies, as if they already knew each other.»

«Elisheva, I don't think we'll ever be able to understand this. It's strange, but in the first few moments after I felt I would have this child, I was able to let go completely. I felt no need to think about how it would happen. It was enough that it is the way it is.»

«That's amazing, Mariam.»

«Yes, but afterwards things no longer went so well. Then came the doubts. Soon, I became quite unbearable due to my fear and desperation. In fact, one of the reasons I started out on this journey to visit you was because I felt I couldn't inflict my moodiness upon my mother any longer. The other reason was that I'd heard from Sarah and Shimon you were also expecting a child — another miracle — so I wanted to share my experience with you.» Mariam paused briefly. «I thought, Elisheva will understand …»

«I do understand, Mariam. And if you tell me you haven't slept with any man, well — I believe you, although it does sound most strange.»

Mariam then felt it was time to move onto a lighter subject. «Have you already thought about how exactly I can help you in the coming months?»

«Indeed I have. Last night in bed, when I couldn't sleep, I thought it all out; the olive harvest will be starting shortly. Normally I'd be doing the harvesting, but now I'd be really grateful if you could take that on. Zecharijas can't help, since his duties as a priest in the temple take up all his time.»

«I'd be pleased to do that. Anything else?»

«I've already got a crib, indeed most things are

already here. Last week, the old wise woman came to see me, the one who lives in a little stone house below Gethsemane. She checked on me and said everything looks fine, but that I must only do light work due to my age. It's my opinion that if God chooses to grant me a child, He'll also take care of it in my womb. But I'll certainly adhere to her directions, more or less.»

«You mustn't take any risks, Elisheva. God is powerful, but we shouldn't shift all responsibility onto Him. We need to stand up for our own actions, or else He can't help us. That's my belief.»

«Yes, you're right, of course, and I will be obedient … more or less …» said Elisheva with an impish grin.

«Right, what else needs to be done? Feed the donkey, milk the goat …»

«I can milk the goat,» interrupted Elisheva. «I always feel that does me good.»

«Alright, and of course there's the house to clean and tidy, that goes without saying. Would you like me to do the cooking? Or would you rather do that yourself»

«Oh yes, I'll do that myself, if you can get the ingredients from the market for me.»

They were deeply absorbed in the organisation of the housework when Zecharijas arrived home. He gave his wife a kiss and looked kindly at Mariam. It was time for the midday meal, which Elisheva prepared whilst Mariam laid the table. Elisheva said the prayer of blessing, and the family ate lunch. After the meal, Zecharijas wrote down the latest news from Jerusalem on his tablet – people were saying that the Romans were considering increasing the number of crucifixions for agitators, as the Zelots were gaining in influence everywhere, causing disruption.

Afterwards, Zecharijas went back to Jerusalem, and the women cleared the table together.

«We're going to have to tell Zecharijas about my pregnancy,» said Mariam despondently.

«Mmh, yes, that's true, but please leave it to me. He'll need time to digest this incredible news, and I don't want you to have to deal with his anger.»

Mariam thanked Elisheva but believed she would have to get used to dealing with her family's anger when telling them about her pregnancy.

On her way back to Sarah and Shimon in the evening, she imagined Elisheva at that very moment telling Zecharijas the news of her pregnancy, and she thought he would probably greet her very differently next day. She felt a great sadness at the complications that had come into her life, and nostalgia for the untroubled days of her youth. So she appreciated the lightness of the atmosphere that evening with Sarah, Shimon and their family, as they laughed at the antics of the children and enjoyed the latest Bethany gossip.

But in bed that night, it occurred to her that as soon as they heard about her pregnancy, the relationship to this family was also going to change.

Meanwhile, Elisheva had indeed spoken with Zecharijas. As expected, he became very angry and even wrote the word „Whore!" on his tablet. He also wrote that Elisheva was naive and gullible, and would believe anything any liar or vagabond dished up to her. But Elisheva's character was strong enough to stand up to her husband's attempts to browbeat her, and she defended Mariam and her own decision to keep her with her for the coming months.

«Even if what you've written were true, she's a strong young woman and I urgently need help. But Mariam is sincere, I can feel it. And I do believe in miracles, since God took away the shame of my own infertility.»

In reply, Zecharijas wrote: «But this business with Mariam is completely against the laws of nature! How can a woman become pregnant without sleeping with a man? It's never happened before, and it's not possible!. She's a liar who wants to worm her way into your confidence, can't you see that? I never wish to see her in this house again!»

«I admit it's against the laws of nature. But Zecharijas, you're a man of God, and a priest in His temple. You read from the Scriptures, for example the section of the Torah where God parted the waters of the Red Sea, to allow our people Israel to walk through it and be saved! Why can you not believe Him to be capable of planting a child in a woman's womb? As a rule, a miracle is something that's never happened before, otherwise it wouldn't be a miracle!»

Zecharijas shook his head sceptically and wrote: «That was in the days of the Patriarchs. But we're living in our time now, and I don't see why our great God, Holy is His Name, should concern Himself with your niece Mariam.»

«I don't believe it's her that's important. It's the child who will be great and a light to glorify our people – that's my belief!» ended Elisheva solemnly and with determination. She could tell that these last words had impressed him more than anything else. Now she would just allow them to sink in. As she had said to Mariam, he needed time. But Elisheva was sure that in the end, he would allow Mariam to stay.

When Mariam came to visit Elisheva next day, she stood faint-heartedly at the door, wanting to put off the moment of discovering Zecharijas' rejection. Elisheva appeared from the stable and called out: «Mariam! Welcome, my dear! Come on in!»

Mariam was relieved to be made welcome so heartily by Elisheva; it seemed promising. She went into the house with her, laying the vegetables and flour from the market on the table.

«I'm so scared!» admitted Mariam. «I hardly dare ask how Zecharijas took the news of my pregnancy yesterday evening.»

Elisheva laid a comforting arm around Mariam's slender shoulder, giving it a squeeze. «Mariam, it went just as one would expect. I'll not beat about the bush: You have every reason to feel anxious. From Zecharijas' reaction, I can well imagine what you're going to be up against when you tell other acquaintances. He hasn't written so much on his tablet for ages! But I told you yesterday that we need to give him time. Be patient and trust that he will come to see the light. God is with us both, and He will help us, I know it.»

«Men can sometimes be so obstinate!» exclaimed Mariam.

«Well, this news is not so easy to digest! You can't expect people to accept it just like that. After all, no woman has ever become pregnant without the participation of a man before, and that's what Zecharijas stressed yesterday evening. He doesn't believe you so far, and for the time being he's even forbidden you to enter this house again. But he's a man of God, and he should know that God can work miracles; that won't be anything new to him.»

«Then I'll try to wait patiently until he feels more kindly towards me. Will you please come and tell me once that happens, Elisheva?»

«Yes, I think that's best at present! I honestly don't think it will take more than one or two days; I know my husband.» Elisheva smiled and brushed a strand of hair from Mariam's worried brow. «God has great plans for our children, and He'll not abandon us. Anyway, I don't give up easily, and I'll continue to beleaguer Zecharijas, until he's ready to make you welcome here again. When he is, I'll come over to Sarah's and fetch you. Alright?»

The two women embraced warmly. Mariam left Elisheva's house with a heavy heart and told Sarah and Shimon that Elisheva still required more time to prepare for her visit. Sara and Shimon were glad to have her company for a while longer, but Mariam was not comfortable deceiving friends like Sarah and Shimon, as it was not in her nature to dissemble.

It did indeed take two more days before Elisheva came to fetch Mariam, who could see from her aunt's beaming face that all was now well. She packed her few possessions, said a grateful farewell to Sarah, Shimon and the family and made her way over to Elisheva's house with a cheerful heart.

On the way, Elisheva told Mariam what had happened. «It always takes a while with him, Mariam, but then he's all enthusiastic!»

«I'm so relieved, and yet I still feel embarrassed about meeting him again.»

«Oh, I do understand that, but you'll see, everything's fine now!»

«However did you go about convincing him, Elisheva? Perhaps I can learn from you how to tell my family.»

«It'll probably be different in each case, Mariam. You see, people are different, and you'll have to find the right words for each one. But I think it was my telling Zecharijas of the importance of your child for the people of Israel that convinced him. You see, he's a priest, so of course he's open to God's greatness and what He can do with and for His people. That may not be the case with other friends, but I'm just as optimistic as far as your mother is concerned.»

«And Jossef?» asked Mariam anxiously.

Elisheva had no reply to that, and her aunt's

worried frown told Mariam that she was aware how difficult the task of telling Jossef would prove to be. Elisheva was glad not to be in Mariam's shoes.

«Oh my, it's so difficult!» exclaimed Mariam. «However am I going to cope with people's reactions in Nazareth? I'm so glad it's still some time away!»

«Exactly,» answered Elisheva. «You need time too, before you're ready to face your family and friends. Here you can build up your strength amongst supportive people. You'll see, everything's going to be alright.»

The women got down to the housework, and the mutual activity lightened their hearts. By the time Zecharijas came home for lunch, the gaity in the house made it easier for Mariam and Zecharijas to meet again. He greeted her just as politely as before, and Mariam felt infinitely relieved that she had been accepted by her relations in spite of her pregnancy. If things had worked out in Bethany, then surely she could hope they would also work out at home in Nazareth, and that was still a long time hence!

In the afternoon, Mariam cleared the table and cleaned the courtyard. She had never been afraid of hard physical work, and now it helped her in body and soul. After the long journey she was healthy and strong, used to plenty of exercise and almost indefatigable. While she worked, she sang softly to herself, and she felt there was an echo from inside her, as if her singing was pleasing to her growing child.

Soon it would be time for the olive harvest. Mariam was looking forward to the work. Elisheva had told her some of her trees were more than 100 years old. Mariam had always felt an affinity to olive trees with their fine silver-green leaves. If there was still enough oil left after the requirements for the household, meals and temple lamps had been met, they agreed that Mariam should take the oil to sell at the local market. Since her work helped Elisheva, it made it doubly pleasing.

Once the courtyard was clean, Mariam came in to sit with Elisheva. The two women drank sweet wine from the earthenware pitcher. After the heat outside, it was beautifully cool in the house, and the work had made Mariam thirsty. It was so comfortable to sit together, drinking and chatting.

«Elisheva, have you already decided on a name for your child?» asked Mariam.

«Indeed I have, he'll be named Jochanan,»

answered Elisheva without hesitation

«Jochanan? Where did you get that name from? No-one in your family's named Jochanan!»

«You're quite right, Mariam, and actually I have yet to discuss it with Zecharijas. But when I got to know of my forthcoming pregnancy, it was as if a small voice was whispering this name to me. I can't explain it any better — you know? When there was that beating of wings and the rush of wind …»

«Oh yes, I understand!»

«And what about your child, Mariam? Do you have a name for it yet?»

«Indeed I do, he'll be named Jeshua.» Mariam also answered without hesitation.

«And where did you get that name from?»

Mariam smiled. «Surely you can guess? The beating of wings, the rush of wind …»

Elisheva laughed. «The name was whispered to you too?»

«Yes, it was. My child will be called Jeshua, and that's final.»

There was a comfortable silence, during which both women were thinking about their children. Through telling each other their names, the children had suddenly become closer and more real.

«Do you also sometimes see your child running about the house in your mind's eye?» asked Elisheva.

«No, I don't, not yet. But then your child has

been in your womb three months longer than mine. And also: This is your house and your child really will be running about in it. That will probably only start happening to me when I'm back home. But it's good that you can already picture your child here!»

Suddenly, the child in Elisheva's womb moved so much that both women saw it. They smiled at each other. Mariam laid a hand on Elisheva's belly but the child was still now. «Your child moves when it wants to, not when I want it to,» said Mariam.

«It's an amazing feeling when the child moves for the first time. But it's never moved so strongly as it did when you first greeted me, Mariam. Our children hear us, they can already feel everything. They're already sharing in our world through us. Will you sing for us again? Please sing that song you were singing in the courtyard just now. It soothed me, and I'm sure it'll soothe our children too!»

Mariam laid one hand on Elisheva's belly and the other hand on her own, and she began to sing:

«You have searched me, Lord, and you know me.
You know when I sit and when I rise;
you perceive my thoughts from afar.
You discern my going out and my lying down;
you are familiar with all my ways.
Before a word is on my tongue, you, Lord, know it completely.
You hem me in behind and before, and you lay

your hand upon me.

Such knowledge is too wonderful for me, too lofty for me to attain.

Where can I go from your Spirit? Where can I flee from your presence?

If I go up to the heavens, you are there; if I make my bed in the depths, you are there.

If I rise on the wings of the dawn, if I settle on the far side of the sea,

even there your hand will guide me, your right hand will hold me fast.

If I say, "Surely the darkness will hide me and the light become night around me,"

even the darkness will not be dark to you; the night will shine like the day, for darkness is as light to you.

For you created my inmost being; you knit me together in my mother's womb.

I praise you because I am fearfully and wonderfully made; your works are wonderful, I know that full well.

My frame was not hidden from you when I was made in the secret place, when I was woven together in the depths of the earth.

Your eyes saw my unformed body; all the days ordained for me were written in your book before one of them came to be.

How precious to me are your thoughts, o God! How vast is the sum of them!

Were I to count them, they would outnumber the grains of sand — when I awake, I am still with you.
Search me, God, and know my heart; test me and know my anxious thoughts.
See if there is any offense in me, and lead me in the way everlasting.[3]»

The lilting melody ended, Mariam's voice ebbed away, and the soft sound of beating wings and the rush of wind faded too.

In the darkness, the two women sat completely still in silent understanding, and time seemed to stand still too. For God, their children were visible, He already knew everything about them. He would guide them on their way in the world and work His will for the world through them. It was really too wonderful for the two women to grasp in depth. But it was enough that they were able to experience it together. All else was in God's hands.

Eventually Elisheva got up and lit an oil lamp, while Mariam made ready for her first night in Elisheva's house. It already felt completely natural, as if she had been living here for ages. Zecharijas came home very late, but by then both women were already sleeping deeply.

_____

[3] Psalm 139

14

One month later, it was time for the olive harvest. Elisheva had spent two days giving Mariam instructions on how to harvest the fruit from the trees, but Mariam was still very glad to see Shimon arrive, offering his help. Mariam carried baskets, hook poles and jute sacking from the stable to the grove. They laid the sacking under the trees and placed the baskets at the edge of the grove. First, they shook the branches with the hook poles, then the fallen olives were raked together and poured into the baskets. Two full baskets were set aside for use in the kitchen and the temple. The rest were to be pressed for oil in a neighbour's mill and then sold at the market. Once all that had been done, Shimon and Mariam climbed up wooden ladders to cut back the branches, at the same time harvesting the remaining olives. The work was strenuous, but Mariam enjoyed it, and she was quick to learn the best way of carrying out the job.

They ended the first harvest day in the late afternoon, after they had finished cutting and harvesting one of the trees. In the meantime, Elisheva had prepared a fine meal, and Shimon joined them to eat a little as he was very hungry. Although Sarah would be cooking for him later, he had quite enough appetite for two meals.

Shimon left, and until Zecharijas arrived home, the two women enjoyed a little peace and quiet, taking the opportunity for a chat.

«Do you know what I keep asking myself, Elisheva? Why ever did God choose us? Why have these special children been planted in our wombs, and not in the wombs of more important women? We're only humble people. What do you think singles us out to receive God's great blessing for this responsibility?»

«God has always moved in mysterious and intricate ways, Mariam. Just look at the history of our people. King David was a humble shepherd boy until he was called to become a leader. Joseph was the youngest son of a nomadic family and became Pharao's trusted vizier. There are so many examples of this in our history. It seems our God has a preference for humble people, maybe because they have no airs and graces – although I'm not so sure about Joseph; he had airs and graces aplenty from a young age, even though he came from a humble background!

But then maybe it's because we belong to the house of Aharon. Your mother and I are both direct descendents, that can be traced way back. And that also means you are a direct descendent of the house of Aharon, and you know how our families have always been raised to follow God's commands. It also means we have a special relationship to the Torah and the scriptures. That inclination is particularly strong in you. Just look at how often you've recited and sung from the Scriptures since you've been here. I'm convinced that has a great influence upon the new life growing inside you. God sees it all, and He's using it for His plan.»

«I've never looked at it that way before,» answered Mariam pensively. Elisheva's wise words touched her heart, and she intended to ponder upon them during the next few days. She got up to put away the pots, standing a little straighter than before. With a more self-assured attitude, she went about her work. When she lay down to sleep, she felt more balanced and centred than she had done for some time.

15

The following day, Shimon brought along a young acquaintance from the neighbourhood named Mordechai, who was going to organise the harvest for his own family as his father had recently died. Assisting at Elisheva's harvest would give him an insight into the process of harvesting olives. Mariam and Shimon gave him instructions and demonstrated the task. He learnt quickly and was soon a real help, meaning that the harvest progressed faster than Mariam could have imagined.

The house now became even more lively, and Elisheva was happy to be entertaining additional guests at table. At lunchtime on the fourth day, young Mordechai explained that his mother was from Nazareth where they also used to have an olive grove. Now that his father had passed away, his mother Rivka wished to return to Nazareth.

«Are you going to accompany your mother to Nazareth, Mordechai? Or do you prefer to stay in Bethany?» asked Elisheva.

«Yes, I'm going to go with my mother. She still needs me. Later, if I want to go away and live elsewhere, I can still do so. But right now it's fine for me to move to Nazareth.»

«When do you plan to leave?»

«Soon after this olive harvest. We're going to begin our harvest a week after I finish here.»

Two days after the Sabbath, when Mariam, Shimon and Mordechai returned to the house from the harvest, Elisheva was looking pale and sitting cramped up against the wall in the corner. Mariam quickly sent the men home and sat down next to her.

«Elisheva, whatever's the matter?»

«I don't know, Mariam – today, I kept having to pass water, and I got such a bad headache that I had to lie down. Just look at my hands, they're all swollen! I must confess, I'm really glad you're here with me.»

«Dearest aunt, I'll wait here with you until Zecharijas comes home, then I'll run over and fetch the wise woman. She can advise us – we don't want to do anything wrong. Please lie down and rest now until I return with her.» Elisheva lay down in her chamber, and soon Zecharijas arrived home. Mariam told him what had happened, then she went in to Elisheva's chamber.

«You're a dear!» exclaimed Elisheva and reached for Mariam's hand. Mariam gave her hand a short squeeze, then she hurried off towards Gethsemane. All the way, she was thinking: «I do hope the wise woman is home!». Soon the little stone house came in sight below the olive grove. Smoke was whisping up from the chimney; Mariam breathed a sigh of relief.

She knocked and entered. The old woman was standing by the stove stirring a pot of soup. «Peace be with you!» called Mariam impatiently and bowed her head briefly. «I've just come from Elisheva in Bethany, she's in her seventh month, and she doesn't seem at all well!»

«Sit down, child!» said the old woman kindly. «What's your name?»

«I'm Mariam, Elisheva's niece from Nazareth. I'm staying with her, and I'd just come home from harvesting the olives. Venerable wise woman, we're both very frightened!»

«Tell me what her symptoms are, Mariam.»

Mariam told her what she knew, but she wished she had taken better note of the details and asked Elisheva more, for she was aware that there was little she could tell her. She also forgot to mention the weak bladder, being too nervous to think properly.

«Mariam, I think I can tell from what you've said what's wrong with Elisheva. It's something that can happen to elderly mothers who have never given birth before. We can help her if she does just as I tell her. I'll prepare some medicine, then I'll come with you right away.»

Mariam heaved another deep sigh of relief, suddenly becoming aware how flatly she had been breathing. It was good to know there was someone there to help them and that they were not alone.

The old woman gave Mariam a beaker of water which she drank greedily, then she went into an adjacent chamber and rummaged around on her shelves for the required medicine, which she packed in a pouch, after which she returned to Mariam in the kitchen.

«Right, child, let's be off!»

16

The two women hurried back to Bethany, Mariam always running a few paces ahead. She wondered what the old woman had put in the pouch, and the old woman answered her as if she had spoken: «The medicine in the pouch will control the pressure of Elisheva's blood. It'll do her good!» Mariam was amazed that the woman had answered a question she had not asked. The old woman laughed and said: «Mariam, you kept looking at the pouch!» Fine, thought Mariam, but she had not posed this second question aloud either! It was somewhat uncanny, but Mariam was impressed. She could feel that she was rapidly gaining confidence in the wise old woman.

At last they arrived at Elisheva's house. She was noticeably worse; Zecharijas was sitting next to his wife moaning with worry. He was obviously very nervous, and that was not going to help Elisheva at all! The old woman shooed him away, sat next to Elisheva, took her hand and chanted a healing mantra until Elisheva started to relax a little. Mariam stood behind them and watched in fascination as the old woman passed her hand over Elisheva's belly, always in the same pattern. She then began to sing a song about motherhood and the child in Elisheva's belly. A refrain followed each verse, and soon Mariam was able to sing along with the refrain, coaxing a weak smile from Elisheva.

Once Elisheva had fully relaxed, the old woman asked about further symptoms. In the meantime, Elisheva had also started to feel some pain in her abdomen, and she explained that her sight had suddenly become blurred.

«These are all typical, known signs,» said the old woman. «When women of your age become pregnant, their bodies sometimes react sensitively to the growing child. I'll now tell you what you need to do: You must rest much more than you have done, lie down often and ensure you sleep plenty. Rest — lie down — sleep,» she chanted, as if to imprint the message on their minds, which indeed it did.

«Then you must eat nuts: almonds, or the seeds of sunflowers are good. Eat nuts – eat nuts,» she chanted.

«You also need to drink much more! That's important, as your symptoms have to do with water: the bladder, the swollen hands holding back the water. Water – drink lots of water!

Then you must see to it that you get enough salt in your food. Salt of life – salt of life!

Take this medicine three times a day: in the morning, at midday and in the evening with a little water. Medicine in the morning – medicine at midday – medicine in the evening!» The old woman was quiet for a while while she massaged Elisheva's belly.

«And now repeat with me:
Rest — lie down — sleep.
Eat nuts.
Drink water, plenty of water.
Salt of life.
Medicine in the morning – medicine at midday – medicine in the evening.»

All three spoke the healing mantra together, so that it was impressed upon them, and they sensed that they had been helped, strengthened and made to feel more secure.

«Elisheva, I'll visit you once a week from now on and see how you're doing,» said the old woman softly. «If you do exactly as I've told you, you have nothing to fear. Any questions?»

«What does the medicine do?» asked Elisheva.

The old woman explained that it was for her blood pressure. «That'll soon help you. Take some right now.» She put a little powder in a beaker and filled it with water. Elisheva drank it and pulled a face. «Yes, yes, I know it doesn't taste too good. But it'll do you good, it'll do you so much good!»

And she started to sing the song of motherhood and the growing child again, Mariam joining in the refrain. A deep peace filled the chamber. The wise woman knew the women would now be able to cope. She took her leave of them and set off on her way back to Gethsemane.

Mariam joined Zecharijas in the kitchen,

placing a beaker of water in front of him and saying: «I don't think we need to worry now. Elisheva's in good hands.» She sat down opposite him and saw that his eyes had filled with tears.

«Mariam, I'm so glad you're here!» he wrote agitatedly on his tablet. «How dreadful it would be to lose my Elisheva now, just when we're finally expecting a child!»

«Have faith, Uncle Zecharijas. God's with you. Through his great love and mercy, he's given you this child; I'm absolutely sure he'll not take it away again.» She laid her hand on his arm. As she stood up to go about her work, she heard him breath in heavily and jerkily, then let out his breath on a long sigh.

17

Elisheva was a compliant patient. She was well aware what was at stake and did not want to take any risks. Mariam now also took on the cooking, and as she was a good cook, no-one had anything against the arrangement. The last three days of the olive harvest were strenuous for her, but she was a strong woman and coped well. The neighbour with the oil mill had already pressed their olives and delivered the oil in large pitchers.

«Tomorrow I must start selling the oil at the market,» said Mariam. «You need to give me exact instructions for that too! I want to know how much I can ask, and I have no idea whether I can offer discounts, or to whom.»

Elisheva and Shimon explained the market sales to Mariam. Next morning, she set off with the oil in the two large clay pitchers, also taking small pitchers with stoppers for decanting. She bound the two large pitchers to either side of the donkey and the small pitchers on a string around her waist. She also carried Elisheva's large leather money pouch. Sarah had agreed to cook for Elisheva and Zecharijas that day, so Mariam could absent herself without having to worry.

It turned out to be a long hard day at the market; Mariam had to be on her guard so as not to be cheated by impertinent customers. She kept her wits about her, and it required some strength of character to hold her ground. The noise was quite deafening, with everyone calling out their wares and the customers shouting too. Mariam proclaimed the quality of her olives with a market cry as strong as the next man's. She had a good voice and was soon noticed by customers who already knew the quality of Elisheva's olives, so that by evening all the oil had been sold and Mariam led the donkey home with a full money pouch and empty pitchers.

When she entered the kitchen, she was pleased to see Elisheva with rosy cheeks, looking much better and happier. The bustle in the house was obviously not doing her any harm, for Shimon, Sarah, Jonah and the children had also arrived, and they were all talking a hundred to the dozen.

«See, Mariam – that's what it's going to be like here in future!» exclaimed Elisheva happily. «And just wait till you hear what Sarah has to tell us!»

Mariam turned inquisitively towards Sarah. «Sarah, what is it?»

«Oh Mariam, I'm expecting too – just imagine, I'm going to have my third child!»

«Sarah, that's wonderful!» exclaimed Mariam, hugging their neighbour warmly. She thought how nice it would be if she could only say that she was also expecting a child! It would not be long now before everyone started to notice anyway, as her gown was beginning to pinch around the waist. Mariam could not imagine how she was going to tell

Sarah without losing her friendship.

After the meal, Sarah and Mariam were alone putting things away in the pantry, and Mariam worked up the courage to say: «Sarah, there's something I want to speak to you about, but we need to find a time when we're not disturbed ...»

Sarah looked surprised. «Now you've got me curious!» she said.

«Please, I don't want to tell you yet, as your whole family are in the kitchen, and you'll be off home shortly. But now the harvest is over and I have more time, I feel the urge to tell you, and I'd really like to do so before the Sabbath. Can I come to you tomorrow? And could you please arrange for us to be alone?»

«Of course!» replied Sarah, laying her hand on Mariam's shoulder. «We'll have a comfortable morning together. I'll see to it that we're not disturbed!»

Mariam was grateful but inwardly she doubted very much that the morning would be comfortable. At least she had broached the subject, and that alone gave her a feeling of relief.

18

Since Elisheva was feeling so much better, Mariam reckoned she could leave her alone for a morning, so she set off with a heavy heart towards Sarah's house. She wished fervently that it was already over. If only she knew that Sarah would not spurn her.

For the first time, Mariam felt a dragging in her lower back. She was beginning to feel the effects of the last weeks of heavy physical work as well as her growing belly. Thank God they had been able to complete the harvest before it became too much for her.

Sarah was awaiting Mariam in front of the house. She came to meet her and embraced her. «Mariam, you look so serious — whatever's worrying you so?»

«Can we please go into the house?» requested Mariam. They went and sat in the kitchen together. As Sarah had promised, they were alone.

«So what's worrying you, Mariam?» She laid a comforting hand on Mariam's arm.

Mariam had no idea how to begin. She stuttered, started to explain, stopped again, looked down at her lap and wrung her long fingers nervously. Her breathing was jerky. She was sweating and red in the face. «Oh God, help me!» she exclaimed suddenly, «Sarah, I'm pregnant!»

Silence filled the room. Sarah sat stock-still, her eyes wide. Sie removed her hand from Mariam's arm. With her elbows on the table, she folded her hands and laid her head in them. «That really is terrible news,» she said flatly.

Mariam could not say another word. Sarah had reacted exactly as she had feared she would. Was it going to be like this with all her friends? Would she end up alone with no help in the world? She knit her brow, and her mouth puckered to a thin line. What would become of her and her child ?

«So you've already slept with your betrothed, before the wedding?»

«The child's not Jossef's,» admitted Mariam.

«What?!» exclaimed Sarah. «No, I don't believe it! When was this? Back in Nazareth? Or was it with someone on our journey? What in heaven's name were you thinking of? I'm sorely tempted to call you a whore, I can tell you.»

Mariam gave a long sigh. «You wouldn't be the first. Zecharijas wrote that word on his tablet, when he heard the news.»

«I'm not surprised, who can blame him?»

«Sarah, I haven't slept with any man.»

«Oh you haven't? So what was it? Magic, or what?» said Sarah ironically.

«I can really understand you not believing me; in your position I don't think I would either. But as you see, I'm still living at Elisheva's und Zecharijas' house, and they're upright godly people. Zecharijas couldn't believe it either, just like you. But Elisheva believed me from the first. She understood that God has worked a miracle upon me.»

«Ah yes? A miracle, huh?»

«Oh Sarah!» squirmed Mariam, «I don't even know myself how it happened! It was as if an angel came to me and I discovered I was to have a child, and that the child would be great, and important for the people of Israel. It's a gift from God, not only for me but for our people.»

«You're kidding me, right?»

«No, Sarah, I really believe it! I've experienced it physically, and I can see I'm going to have to live with the fact that people will spurn me, although I've done nothing wrong. For some reason, God has chosen me to bear this child without conception by a man. Believe me, I would have preferred it if He could have waited until I was married to Jossef. But it seems He wanted it this way; apparently it has to happen like this!»

Sarah was silent, attempting to assimilate this unbelievable news. Mariam had really given her something hard to digest. Although Mariam did not seem to be the type of girl to sleep around before marriage, it just seemed impossible. Such a thing had never happened – it could not happen. Could it?

«I'm very fond of you, Mariam, otherwise I'd already have thrown you out of my house. But I do find it very, very difficult to believe what you're telling me. What's so special about you, that God should choose you for such a thing?»

«Believe me, I've asked myself the same question!» exclaimed Mariam. «I can give you no other answer than the one Elisheva gave me: Throughout the history of our people, humble folk have often been used as instruments of God. Even King David was previously a shepherd boy. But perhaps it's because I'm of the lineage of Aharon. Our families have always been brought up to have a special relationship to the Torah. Elisheva reckons that could have an influence on the baby growing inside me. God sees that, and He'll use it for His plan.»

«Mariam, you'll have to give me time. I can't just accept that you've become pregnant by a miracle, that's asking too much of me. I will ponder it in my heart though, and when I'm ready I'll come to you, alright?»

Mariam realised that Sarah was making a considerable concession. She nodded slowly. «Yes, Sarah. I do understand your reservations, indeed I'd have them too. I can only repeat that I'm sincere. This is no white lie. What I've told you is absolutely true.»

«Go now, please, and leave me to think about it in peace.»

«Farewell, Sarah, I hope you'll want to see me again.»

«I hope so too. Goodbye, Mariam.»

19

Mariam dragged herself sadly back to Elisheva's house. Elisheva could tell that Mariam was suffering. «Where have you been, Mariam?»

Mariam sighed. «I went to see Sarah.»

«You've told her about your pregnancy.» It was a statement, not a question.

«She hasn't spurned me completely yet.»

«That's good. It'll be like that with a lot of people, they'll need time, just as Zecharijas did.»

«Yes, but Sarah has no Elisheva who'll speak up for me and convince her!»

«You'll be able to do that yourself, Mariam. Be patient, it'll turn out alright in the end! Sarah's fond of you, and she's a woman of faith with a quick mind.»

«Is a quick mind helpful in a case like this, Elisheva?»

«No, you're right of course. It isn't really helpful. But God's angels will convince her somehow. You need to be strong and patient, and leave it up to our God!»

Sarah didn't even take two days, as Zecharijas had done. Next day in the late afternoon she came storming in and embraced Mariam warmly.

«I still can't understand what you've told me, Mariam — but I'm fond of you and I need you as a friend. I can't abandon you!»

Mariam's tears of relief flowed freely, dripping

from her chin onto Sarah's shoulder. «Thank you!» she said simply, giving Sarah a warm hug. «I was so afraid of losing you, but I just had to tell you.»

«When you were being sick on the journey — was that because you were pregnant?»

«Yes, of course. I would have liked to have told you straight away, but I wasn't even sure myself at the time that I was pregnant.»

«You poor soul! You were in a very difficult position. You're going to find that a lot of people won't believe you, just as I couldn't to begin with.»

«I know, Sarah. And then there's Jossef to tell! I've discussed it with Elisheva. I'm going to have to be very strong. God has set me a hard task.»

Mariam swallowed heavily, and Sarah looked at her with great concern.

20

Elisheva's child was moving in her womb more often now. The wise old woman came once a week as promised, to check that the child was lying correctly and that all was well with the mother-to-be. She had had no further negative reactions, and in one more month it would be time for the birth. As soon as Elisheva's labour started, Mariam was to go and fetch the wise woman.

The house was filled with excitement, which also affected Zecharijas. He prayed fervently for Elisheva and their child, all the while attempting to act as a faithful man of God should, but only managing to convey an edgy nervousness. He felt far more powerless than the women and was well tired of waiting.

Elisheva glanced at her husband and winked at Mariam, who smiled understandingly. The waiting was indeed difficult to cope with — she felt just the same.

«I believe he's just pulling himself together for your sake. If I were alone with him, I think he'd be unbearable!» whispered Elisheva.

Mariam laughed. «Oh yes, it's specially difficult for the men! They've done their part, and can't do any more.»

Elisheva joined in her laughter. «In your case, Mariam, that's not even true!»

Mariam was on the brink of feeling embarrassed by her words, but then she laughed loudly, and it was liberating not to take the whole situation so seriously for once. The most difficult part still lay ahead of her, namely telling Jossef. The grimness of her situation would raise its ugly head again soon enough, but for the moment this levity was healing.

«What are you two laughing about?» wrote Zecharijas on his tablet.

«Nothing!» they both answered together.

«I'm glad to see you're coping so well,» he wrote. Some of his nervousness left him with the women's unburdened laughter. It comforted him. A little of the tension had left the room and that helped them all.

Zecharijas prepared some oil to take to the temple next day, while the women busied themselves in the kitchen.

Then he wrote on his tablet: «I've heard that Mordechai and his mother won't leave for Nazareth quite as early as planned. They're only leaving in one and a half months from now.»

«That's good!» said Elisheva. «Rivka will have more time to prepare for moving. It's challenging to move to another town without a husband.»

«Mordechai will be a great help to her though. He's become very responsible, and is turning out to be a fine young man,» added Mariam.

***

A few days later, Elisheva asked: «Mariam, how much longer do you think you'll stay with us?»

«Oh, Aunt Elisheva, I'd just love to stay here forever, but I'm well aware that it's mainly because I'm dreading telling people about my pregnancy when I get home. But I'm looking forward to holding my mother in my arms again and telling her about my pregnancy, even though it will be hard to do.»

«You mustn't forget that the journey will soon become difficult for you. It's better that you leave quite soon, before it becomes uncomfortable to undertake such a long journey on foot, as your body will become heavier by the day from now on.»

«Yes, you're right, I can feel it myself already. But I'm not leaving until you've given birth, and I'd really prefer to stay until after the circumcision and naming.»

«Yes, I think that would be realistic. Let's say you'll be leaving as soon as Jochanan has been given his name.»

«I'll need to find a group with whom I can travel. I have an idea — I think I'll ask Mordechai and Rivka whether I can travel with them.»

«Oh yes! With their new arrangements, that could work out nicely! Go and speak to them straight away. I'm pretty sure they'll be glad of another person to travel in their little group. There's safety in numbers, after all!»

21

Two weeks later Elisheva's confinement began. She cried out, opening her eyes wide and catching her breath at the sudden pain.

«Elisheva!» exclaimed Mariam, «Now it's starting! Remember to breathe like the wise old woman told you — in, pff — out, pff, — in, pff — out, pff!»

Elisheva puffed out a deep breath, grabbed at Mariams hand and pressed it hard.

«Now just keep that up. Remember to breathe deeply and evenly, keep up the breathing and ignore the pain. Go with your breath! I'll run as fast as I can to fetch the wise woman. Will you be alright?»

«I don't know, Mariam — I hope so!»

«Right, Aunt, off I go!»

Mariam ran like the wind over to Gethsemane. The old woman was home; she packed her bundle with the things she required for the birth and hurried after Mariam to Bethany. Mariam had not taken at all long to get to Gethsemane and back. The old woman asked her to fetch hot water and towels, and together they positioned Elisheva ready for the birth.

The old woman took one of the towels and wiped Elisheva's sweating brow. Her whole body was covered in sweat, and in the meantime her labour pains were coming in ever shorter intervals. The old woman checked the position of the child and looked to see how far the neck of Elisheva's womb had already opened, all the while finding time for comforting words, chants and an encouraging touch.

«Elisheva, everything's fine,» she said. «You'll soon give birth.»

Between loud screams, Elisheva smiled gratefully. She was a strong woman for her age, but she needed all her strength to bear the extreme pains of labour. Only the thought of Jochanan's life kept her from despairing, causing her to breathe and push bravely.

After what felt like an eternity, a small dome appeared from Elisheva's womb. More and more of the little head became visible, then the child began to bellow with all his might. Elisheva fell back exhausted onto her pallet. The old woman bound off the umbilical cord and laid the child upon Elisheva's breast. Elisheva cried with exhaustion and relief as she held the little miracle in her arms and smiled rapturously up at Mariam.

«You did so well, Aunt Elisheva!» said Mariam softly, and kissed her aunt on the top of her head. The old wise woman made room for them to share their mutual joy, clearing up around them.

«You've produced a strong lad there!» she said. «What will be his name?»

«Jochanan,» said Elisheva, and repeated the name happily, gazing in awe at her son.

Zecharijas came home that evening to hear their new baby crying. He approached Elisheva with tears of gratefulness and amazement in his eyes, sank to his knees and laid a hand on his son's head in blessing. «God is good,» he wrote, holding up the simple message for Elisheva to read. The little family was now complete. Mariam moved aside to make room for Zecharijas at his wife's side.

22

All around the neighbourhood, the news spread like wildfire that Elisheva had born a son. On the Sabbath, it was the main topic of conversation outside the synagogue. Everyone wanted to come and see the new child, and to pay their respects. The first ones to arrive were Sarah, Shimon, Jonah and the children. Then Rivka and Mordechai and other neighbours came bringing presents, so there was a great coming and going, and no more peace to be had in the house. Everyone praised God for the gift of new life and shared in Elisheva's joy.

Mariam knew in the back of her mind that the day of her departure was now drawing near, but she had no time to think of it as Elisheva needed help with the child, thus enabling her to greet and entertain all the well-wishers. Holding the child in her arms gave Mariam a delightfully warm feeling.

Eight days after the birth, the mohel[4] and his assistant arrived with a sharpened knife to perform the ceremony. All the neighbours had been invited to share in it. Once the cut had been made and the child had voiced his displeasure at this manhandling with a gusty cry, the mohel asked: «What's his name to be?»

Elisheva paused for rather longer than usual,

---

[4] The person carrying out the circumcision

then she said quietly: «He's to be named Jochanan.»

«I beg your pardon?» asked the mohel. «I think I must have misunderstood. Would you please repeat that?»

«He's to be named Jochanan,» repeated Elisheva.

Everyone looked surprised, since no-one in the family was named Jochanan. «Zecharijas needs to be in agreement. It should be his decision,» they suggested to Elisheva.

The mohel asked for Zecharijas to be given his tablet so that he could write down the name he wanted for his son. Shimon fetched the wax tablet and the stylus and gave them to Zecharijas, who wrote in large clear letters: «His name is Jochanan!»

In the general hullabaloo that followed, only Elisheva noticed that Zecharijas was suddenly able to speak again. Softly, so that only Elisheva and Mariam could here it, he said: «God has done everything according to his will, Holy is his name.»

He then stood up. Everyone turned to look at him as he spoke loudly and solemnly, as though he had never lost his voice: «God has done everything according to his will, Holy is his name!»

«Zecharijas!» exclaimed Shimon, «You can speak again!»

«That's also his will. The Lord gives, and the Lord takes away,» replied Zecharijas quietly and humbly.

The guests stared in wonder at Zecharijas. Fear was written on some of the faces because of the strange happenings at this circumcision. Suddenly everyone was in a hurry to return home; the house now seemed uncanny to them.

On their way, the guests told those who had not been invited what had happened, who in turn passed on the news to their relations and friends until the story was soon being told by the gossips all around Jerusalem.

Zecharijas, Elisheva and Mariam were left alone with little Jochanan. His father took the child in his arms, stood in the middle of the room and, above the faint sound of beating wings and rushing wind, he chanted:

«Praise be to the Lord, the God of Israel,
because he has come to his people and redeemed them.
He has raised up a horn of salvation for us
in the house of his servant David
(as he said through his holy prophets of long ago),
salvation from our enemies
and from the hand of all who hate us —
to show mercy to our ancestors
and to remember his holy covenant,
the oath he swore to our father Abraham:
to rescue us from the hand of our enemies,
and to enable us to serve him without fear
in holiness and righteousness before him all our

days.
And you, my child, will be called a prophet of the Most High;
for you will go before the Lord to prepare the way for him
to give his people the knowledge of salvation through the forgiveness of their sins,
because of the tender mercy of our God,
by which the rising sun will come to us from heaven
to shine on those living in darkness and in the shadow of death,
and to guide our feet into the path of peace.[5]»

---

[5] Luke 1, 68-79

23

Two days after the circumcision, Mariam slowly began to pack her bundle, as Rivka had come to tell her that they would be leaving in three days' time. Mariam swallowed heavily as she looked at Elisheva, Zecharijas and Jochanan. Both the child and Zecharijas' voice were still so new and yet already familiar, making it especially difficult to leave. However, she knew she could not keep putting off her departure.

When she had left Nazareth, it had been an escape – an escape from her own self and from her secret. She had felt light, finding everything exciting and not fully realizing the true extent of what was happening to her. Now she was returning to carry her responsibility and she felt heavy and lonely. Although she was glad of Rivka's and Mordechai's escort, they could only offer her protection against physical dangers.

Mariam sat down to eat her last sabbath meal with Elisheva and Zecharijas, but she could hardly swallow a thing. Her heart was heavy in her breast. Elisheva was also very quiet and could not find the right words to lighten their parting. All three went early to bed since they did not wish to prolong the heavy hour any further than necessary.

Next morning, Rivka and Mordechai arrived with three heavily packed donkeys to collect Mariam, who felt that her heart would break. She was unable to speak, she could only stretch out her hand to her hosts of the last three months and weep. Elisheva hugged her tightly. «My girl, you'll be fine!» she said. «You've watched how it went with me. And with you, it won't be so hard, because you're younger.»

Mariam picked up her bundle and followed Rivka and Mordechai down the path. Before the house was hidden from view behind the olive grove, she looked back one last time. The memory of Elisheva with her child in her arms would accompany her for a long time, almost tearing her apart with longing.

24

Rivka and Mordechai had a much faster walking pace than Shimon and Sarah had done. Mariam was hardly able to keep up, partly because she was dragging her feet with dread, but also because her belly made walking far more strenuous than before. Rivka and Mordechai were patient with her, but they did not adapt their pace, since they had a lot to do in Nazareth and wished to make good headway.

The journey provided them with several uncomfortable and difficult situations, as any journey will do, but after only a week they had already passed Mount Tabor and were finally approaching Nazareth again.

Now Mariam began to feel nervous at the thought of her mother seeing her pregnant for the first time, but she was even more frightened at the prospect of meeting Jossef again. She had not thought of him for some time and had been quite successful in suppressing any consideration of this most challenging encounter, but now it was foremost in her mind.

«Do you want to continue to your house alone?» asked Rivka, «or would you like us to accompany you?»

«No, thank you!» replied Mariam. «I'd like to be alone when I see my mother for the first time after so long. But thank you for the offer, and thank you so much for your company on the journey!

You've needed to be very patient with me.»

«Of course, no problem. That goes without saying in your condition! All the best, dearest Mariam, and do come and visit us with your husband and your child, won't you?»

«I certainly will! Goodbye!» Mariam had never broached the subject of her civil status to Rivka and was not intending to do so just as they took their leave. She embraced Rivka, bowed slightly to Mordechai and approached her mother's house with a heavy gait.

25

How well a mother can feel just what is happening to her child, even when she is far away! Mariam had been away for so long, and Hannah had born the three-month separation bravely, often crying herself to sleep. She had longed for the day when Mariam would return to her, but all the time she had had a feeling she was in for a surprise when she did see her daughter again. Mariam had acted so strangely before she left, but Hannah could not make head or tail of why that might be, so she had simply tried to be patient and hoped that all would be well.

When Mariam finally arrived that afternoon, so clearly pregnant, Hannah ran to her and took her in her arms. She was certainly surprised to see Mariam in that state. She sobbed violently, not because of the pregnancy (that conversation could wait), but because she was overwhelmed at finally having her precious daughter back. Now and again, she had been filled with dread that something truly terrible had happened to Mariam and had feared she would never see her again.

«Oh Mariam, oh my darling child! You're back! God be praised! I've missed you so.»

Mariam was crying too, infinitely grateful that her mother had not sent her pregnant daughter packing, even though she did not yet have any knowledge of the situation. Only now did Mariam realise how much she had missed her mother. She felt the warmth of her presence deep in her heart and soul.

«Imma!» she sobbed. «Just look at the state of me! I've got so much to tell you.»

«Let's go inside, my little lamb,» said Hannah, taking her daughter by the hand and leading her into the room where everything had started, with the beating of wings and the rush of wind.

At first, Mariam could only sit there and cry her heart out. Hannah waited patiently with a furrowed brow and knotted fingers. It tore at her heart to see her daughter so distraught. Finally, Mariam began to explain, stuttering tentatively at first, but gradually gaining strength as the story unfolded, until she announced to her mother: «My child will be great among the people of Israel. God intends it to be so. He sent His angel to proclaim it to me. I know it, mother; it's just as I've told you. Can you believe me? Please, please tell me you do!»

«I don't know, Mariam. This is all so new for me. Such a thing's never happened before, you know.»

Mariam had to exert a lot of self-control not to let out a sigh. How many times had she already heard those words! But she knew she had to learn to be patient with those she told, even with her own mother, who also required time to accept the situation.

«Yes, Imma, I know I'm asking a lot of you. Just

sleep on it, and we'll talk again tomorrow.»

Mariam did not feel perfectly satisfied as she lay down to sleep on her mat. Coming home should feel better than this. But what had she expected? Had she thought her mother would understand immediately? That would be too much to expect of anyone. She was aware that she was being unrealistic. Yet the bitter feeling stayed with her as she tried to sleep.

26

Hannah acted lovingly towards Mariam next morning, but they carefully avoided the subject of the pregnancy. After washing, they spoke the blessing then ate their flat-bread and drank the rich, pure water from the springs around Nazareth. Mariam noticed how much she had missed this good water. There were many things about Nazareth that she only really appreciated since she had been away.

Suddenly she realised she had so far not been spurned by anyone whom she had told of her pregnancy. In her situation, that did not go without saying, but she had only ever noticed how unpleasant it had been to have to explain the situation and that to begin with, no-one had believed her. Even with Elisheva she had felt a slight hesitance when she had first told her, although that had very soon been disappeared. But now she saw that in the end, every single person had stood by her.

«Imma, before I left for Bethany — well, I was a bit of a cow, wasn't I? I think we were both quite glad when I left.»

Hannah smiled. «Well, you certainly weren't very easy to get on with. And I do admit that when you first left, I felt a certain relief at no longer having to put up with your moods. But that soon changed, and I missed you so much that I'd have gladly put up with the worst of your moods only to have you back.

It's wonderful to have you here again, Mariam!»

«And I'm so sorry about my awful moods, but I just couldn't help it. I couldn't understand what was happening to me. I actually couldn't stand myself!»

Hannah kissed her gently. «When are you going to Jossef, Mariam? He misses you too, you know.»

«Really?» asked Mariam diffidently. «Do you think I should go to him already?»

Hannah nodded and stroked her daughter's hair. «After all, he won't bite you,» she said, although she did not feel as confident as she sounded. «Go to him straight after the Sabbath.»

Mariam stayed away from the synagogue on the Sabbath. Next day, she kept finding things she had to do before going to see Jossef, but in the end she gave herself a mental push, as she knew that delaying was not going to help.

She stood at the door of Jossef's workshop and knew that the critical moment had now arrived. Everything she now said would carry weight and may decide upon their future.

Sie stept into the room and started to speak: «Jossef, I ...»

Jossef just stared at her, seeing the way her belly strained beneath her gown. His face reddened to a deep violet, then turned white. His hands cramped around the plane he was holding. All at once, he threw it with full force against the wall, then he turned on his heel away from Mariam and sobbed tensely in his throat. After a couple of seconds, he turned back to Mariam with an expression she had never seen on him before.

«Whose – is – that?» he forced out from between clenched teeth, pointing at her belly. «What's the meaning of this? How dare you come to me in your condition?»

Mariam had never seen Jossef react with such violent feeling. He, who had built the best houses in Nazareth and who was preparing to build a future for the two of them, had always seemed so rational and composed, but now he had completely lost control.

«Mariam, I – I was looking forward to a good life for us both, and now you've ruined everything. I was looking forward so much to the wedding, I loved you …» He forced out the last words, then turned his back on her again, so that she would not see how he fought back the tears. His shoulders shook, and he clenched his fists.

Sometimes, Mariam had wondered whether Jossef really was fond of her or whether he was just marrying her for pratical reasons. He was quite a lot older than her after all. But now, now that it was too late — now she realized how much he had loved her. Her world collapsed around her, as his world obviously had too.

Without having spoken another word, Mariam

turned and quickly left the room. She hurried out of the house and back home to Hannah, walking past her mother without saying a word and going straight into her bedroom, from which she did not appear again that day.

27

Jossef should have been visiting a construction manager at a building site. He also should have delivered a table to a customer. But he was now so confused that he was unable to think straight. He went over to the earthenware pitcher and poured himself a beaker of sweet wine, which he drank in one gulp. He could not visit anybody in his present state.

«I've always been fair to Mariam,» he thought, «how could she deceive me so?»

Then came thoughts of revenge. He imagined how he would expose Mariam in front of the neighbours, and how they would offer him their sympathy. Mariam would creep away like a whipped dog.

He could not bear to stay in the workshop, but he was in no fit state to visit his customers either. He took a staff and went out into the streets of Nazareth. Luckily no-one was around, as they would have noticed immediately that something was wrong. He felt drawn to the fields and hills around Nazareth, where he wandered for hours thinking about his dilemma. What should he do? He did not really wish to expose Mariam, that was just in the heat of his first anger. To let off steam, he had imagined all the names he would call her. But of course he would never really do such a thing.

He would probably just have to break off their

engagement quietly. She would have to leave Nazareth, that was clear. After all, she was at fault. He had his business to think of. At the thought of the future that could have been theirs, he bellowed like a bull and threshed at the ground with his staff until the thick staff broke in two. A sob escaped him, he went down on his knees and cried like a baby with his face in the dust.

As he lay on the ground, he heard a sound like the beating of wings or the rush of wind. The air suddenly seemed to become denser. He lifted his head off the ground and saw a blurred figure a few feet away from him.

«Jossef!» he heard someone call. Was it the figure who had said it, or did the voice come from inside himself? «There's no need to be afraid. Mariam is still your betrothed, and she has not slept with any man.»

«But she's pregnant,» interposed Jossef, perplexed.

The rush of wind increased in volume, sounding like a voice which said: «What she has conceived is a gift from God. The child has come into being through the spirit of God. No man was involved.»

Jossef looked up in confusion, with a deep crease between his brows. He shook his head. «That can't be. Such a thing has never happened before. It can't happen.»

The voice continued as if he had not spoken – and indeed, maybe he had not spoken, maybe he had only thought the words. «Mariam will bear a son, and you will call him Jeshua.»

«Jeshua?» asked Jossef, taken aback.

«Jeshua – Redemption, for he will save his people. The people are misled like a herd of scattered sheep; they err in their ways. Jeshua will save them from their sins. Do you know why this is happening, Jossef?»

«No! I can't understand it at all!»

«All this is happening so that the prophecy will be fulfilled: *The virgin will conceive and give birth to a son, and they will call him Immanuel.*[6] Do you know what the name means, Jossef? Immanuel means 'God with us'. One more thing, Jossef – you may not sleep with Mariam until she has born this child.»

Jossef awoke, as if from a dream. Meanwhile it had become dark; he had lost all sense of time. He felt as if he had only been lying on the ground for an hour, yet half the day had gone.

As much as he had been repelled from Mariam before, now he was driven to find her, for he recognised that whatever he had just experienced, whether a dream or a vision, held the truth. He longed to go to his betrothed, but it was nightfall.

---

[6] Isaiah 7, 14

Now he would have to wait until the next day.

He went home, lay down on his mat and slept deeply and dreamlessly until morning.

28

Hannah awoke early and went into the kitchen. She had hoped that Mariam would have come out of her chamber by now, but it was still completely silent as if she was not even in the house. Hannah looked quietly into her daughter's bedroom and saw that Mariam was lying on her back with empty eyes that seemed to see nothing. «Mariam», she said softly, but her daughter did not react in any way. Hannah was seriously worried – whatever had happened with Jossef to make her cut herself off so completely from reality?

Mariam had reached a very dark place; it seemed to her that she had been going through a long tunnel which became darker and darker, with no chance of escaping. Now she was unable to find the way out. She doubted everything, most of all herself.

Hannah left her daughter to lie there for an hour and pondered what she could do to help her, but she had no idea. Then she heard steps outside the house, opened the door and saw Jossef.

«Jossef!» she called in desperation «Whatever in the world has happened between you and Mariam? My daughter no longer reacts to anything! It's as if she's disappeared from the world.»

Jossef pushed past Hannah, storming directly into Mariam's bedroom. He saw her lying there with her empty eyes turned upwards, unseeing. The small dome of her belly looked so defenceless that he knelt down next to her and placed his rough hands protectively around it. Mariam felt the power flow from Jossef to herself and her child. She turned her head slowly towards him and saw in his eyes that everything had changed. He would now stand by her – all was not lost after all. She slowly lifted a hand and Jossef laid his face in her palm, saying: «My wife!» Then he lifted her up, cradling her in his lap and rocking her like a child until she fell asleep, utterly exhausted from despair.

Hannah looked in on them, saying: «Thank God! We nearly lost both Mariam and the child. It was almost too much for her.» She then left the couple alone and returned to the kitchen.

When Mariam awoke again, Jossef stroked her head and placed his large hand at the back of her neck. «My wife!» he said again and kissed her softly. She returned the kiss just as gently, for it seemed to them both that their situation was still very brittle.

«Why did you come back to me, Jossef? You were so angry. I expected you to send me away. I was convinced you were going to do so.»

«Mariam – you're right, I would have done. I fled, I couldn't face seeing anybody. But while I was out in the hills, there was such an extraordinary atmosphere. It was as if I were looking at a being made of dense air, who spoke to me, like an angel.»

«Was there a sound?» asked Mariam.

«Yes, there was. It sounded something like the beating of wings and the rush of wind.»

«When I discovered that this child was going to be conceived in my womb, I heard the same sounds. I also called it the visit of the angel, as I knew no better way to describe it. For me, it was just as hard as it is for you, Jossef. I wanted to tell my mother, but I didn't know how. I became completely insufferable and just wanted to get away, to be with Elisheva, because she's pregnant too and I thought she'd understand. While I was with Elisheva, I heard the same sounds, and so did she. Do you know what I think? We call it an angel, but I believe that's what happens when the Divine takes possession of us. It makes us into better people — into what we were born to be.»

«We must get married soon, Mariam. I don't want you to become the talk of Nazareth – for your sake, but also for Jeshua's sake.»

«You – know his name?»

«The angel told me. You too?»

«Yes!» Mariam glowed with happiness. That was the greatest gift of all, a wedding present from the angel. Now they shared an experience which would bind them together and which no-one could take from them. Mariam had regained a rock-solid belief in a future with Jossef, and she was looking forward to the wedding. But above all, she was longing for the birth of Jeshua, God's gift, her son!

List of Characters:

Mariam (Mary), the mother-to-be of Jeshua (Jesus) in Nazareth

Elisheva (Elisabeth), the mother-to-be of Jochanan (John) in Bethany

Jossef (Joseph), a carpenter and Mariam's betrothed in Nazareth

Hannah (Anna), Mariam's mother

Zecharijas (Zacharias), Elisheva's husband, and a priest in the temple at Jerusalem

Sarah and Shimon, their children Martha and Elazar (Lazarus), and Shimons father Jonah, neighbours of Elisheva in Bethany

Rivka and her son Mordechai, owners of an olive grove in Bethany

The wise old woman, a midwife in Gethsemane

Stephanie Meier: **Flight to Egypt**

The newly-weds Mariam and Jossef leave Nazareth to register for the census in Jossef's place of origin, Bethlehem, where their child Jeschua is born. In the middle of the night, they make their escape, as King Herod is out to kill their child.

A novel following the biblical account – to be found in the gospel of Matthew, and in the gospel of Luke which differs slightly. Legends from the Coptic-Christian tradition of Egypt also influenced this novel.

Published in October 2021